You Weren't With Me

Chandra Ghosh Ippen

illustrations by Erich Ippen Jr.

Piplo
productions
San Francisco, CA
Piploproductions.com

First edition published in 2019
ISBN: 978-1-950168-02-6 (paperback edition)
ISBN: 978-1-950168-01-9 (hardcover edition)

Summary: Little Rabbit and Big Rabbit are together after a difficult separation, but even though they missed each other, Little Rabbit is not ready to cuddle up and receive Big Rabbit's love. Little Rabbit needs Big Rabbit to understand what it felt like when they were apart. "Sometimes I am very mad. I don't understand why you weren't with me," says Little Rabbit, "I worry you will go away again." Big Rabbit listens carefully and helps Little Rabbit to feel understood and loved. This story was designed to help parents and children talk about difficult separations, reconnect, and find their way back to each other.

Special thanks to colleagues at the Child Trauma Research Program and the National Child Traumatic Stress Network who provided feedback and support.

For families who have experienced difficult separations.
We hope this book helps you talk about your
experiences and brings you closer.

Little Rabbit sighed a deep sigh and said, "When you weren't with me, I missed you so much."

"I missed you too," responded Big Rabbit tenderly. "I thought about you every day."

"I wanted you to hold me,"
said Little Rabbit.

"I wanted to hug you and never let you go," sighed Big Rabbit.

"But you weren't there," whispered Little Rabbit.

Big Rabbit took a deep breath and replied,
"I'm so sorry I wasn't with you.
We are together now."

Little Rabbit thought for a
while and finally spoke.

"Yes, but . . . "

"Sometimes I am very mad. I don't understand why you weren't with me."

"I worry you will go away again."

"My tummy hurts."

"I don't trust you. I feel scared."

"When I am upset,
I need you.
But then I get mad,
and I push you away.

I don't know what to do."

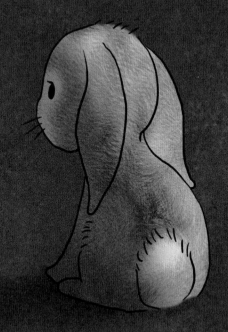

Big Rabbit listened carefully and then softly said, "I am very sorry and very sad that this happened. I wasn't with you, and you didn't understand why."

"You probably felt . . . .

Confused

Scared

Hurt   Sad

Angry

You probably
felt so alone."

"I did," exclaimed Little Rabbit. "I felt so . . .

Alone

Confused

Hurt

Sad

I didn't know
where you were."

Scared

Angry

"Where were you?"
asked Little Rabbit.

Big Rabbit remembered and then shared from the heart. "I wasn't with you, but I was thinking about you all the time.

I hoped and planned and dreamed and worked, so I could get back to you because you are so important, and I love you so much."

"It took a long time," said
Little Rabbit softly.

"Too long," agreed Big Rabbit.

"I don't know what it was like for you when I wasn't there," Big Rabbit added.
"But I want to know.

I want to know what you did.

I want to know if there were good people who helped you.

I want to know if bad or scary things happened too.

I want to give you all the hugs and kisses that I couldn't give you then."

"I wasn't with you then,"
said Big Rabbit.
"But I am here now."

Little Rabbit and Big Rabbit were quite
close now. They looked into each
other's eyes and then said,
"We are together again after so long."

Chandra combines her love of story and cute creatures with her training in clinical psychology. She has co-authored over 20 publications related to trauma and diversity-informed practice and has over 10 years of experience conducting trainings nationally and internationally. In her role as a clinician, supervisor, and the Director of Dissemination and Implementation of Child-Parent Psychotherapy, she works to support families who have been impacted by traumatic separations. She hopes this book and the rabbits help families to talk about difficult separations and reconnect.

As a boy, Erich was always interested in cartoons and character design. In his professional career, he has created visual effects for movies like Rango, Harry Potter, The Avengers, Star Wars and many others. He is also a singer, songwriter, music producer and founding member of the local San Francisco band, District 8.

For more information about the impact of stressful
and traumatic events on children and how grown-ups can help
please visit nctsn.org

For more information about the stories and additional resources
please visit piploproductions.com

Made in the USA
Columbia, SC
11 December 2019